The
Magnificen...
and the Terrible
Toddler

LITTLE DIGMOOR C.P. SCHOOL
ABBEYSTEAD
SKELMERSDALE
LANCS. WN8 9NF
TEL: (01695) 724539

02695

Ma Vile

Vince Vile

Keith and Timothy Elastic

Barrington Small

Fabian Farquar

Hodge the
Little Horror

Seymour Potts

Elsie Potts
(and Gladys)

The Magnificent Misfits and the Terrible Toddler

J.J. MURHALL

Illustrated by
Eleanor Taylor

BLOOMSBURY
CHILDREN'S
BOOKS

This book is dedicated to
Michael and Saoirse Ruby,
and to all those 'misfits'
I have ever known,
including the most 'magnificent'
one of all – Alfie.

XX

All rights reserved; no part of this publication may be
reproduced or transmitted by any means, electronic, mechanical,
photocopying or otherwise, without the prior permission
of the publisher

First published in Great Britain in 1998
Bloomsbury Publishing Plc, 38 Soho Square, London, W1V 5DF

Copyright © Text J. J. Murhall 1998
Copyright © Illustrations Eleanor Taylor 1998

The moral right of the author has been asserted
A CIP catalogue record of this book is available from the
British Library

ISBN 0 7475 3869 7

Printed in England by Clays Ltd, St Ives plc

10 9 8 7 6 5 4 3 2 1

Cover design by Michelle Radford

One

'I WANT THE WORLD! I WANT THE WORLD!!' The ear-piercing wail of Hodge the Little Horror shook the planet Ghastly, echoed around the universe and bounced off the earth. Hodge gripped the bars of his playpen and shook them crossly.

'Don't touch those,' said his mum firmly. 'You'll set the alarm off.'

Hodge stuck his tongue out at her but his mum ignored him. Hodge was a spoilt little brat and whatever Hodge wanted, Hodge usually got. His toy box was so big, it had now been classified as a planet. Attached to a long chain, it floated high above Ghastly, stuffed with so many toys it was overflowing, and now Hodge was after the world to add to his collection.

He stuck his bottom lip out sulkily. 'I'm bored. Uncle Vince says the world would be a great place to play with. *He* says that all you need to do to own the world is to get your hands on the Magnificent Misfits' jar of pickled onions and then you're in business.'

Hodge's mum sighed. 'Your Uncle Vince is a megalomaniac. Take no notice of him,' she replied, referring to Vince Vile, her terrible cousin, who was a master of disguise and all-round bad guy. 'Anyway, I bought you that lovely comet last week. Can't you play with that instead?' she added, checking the padlocks on the specially constructed roof of his playpen. Hodge's mum wasn't taking any chances. Her son was never to be trusted and if he was in a mood, and managed to escape, goodness knows what might happen.

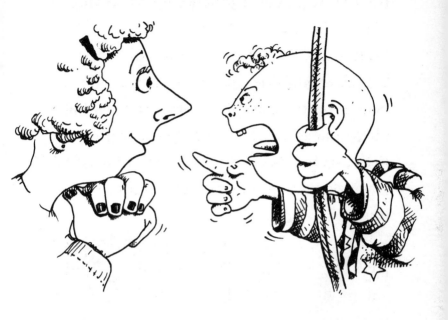

Hodge stamped his foot. 'It's too hot to play with. And if Uncle Vince is a megawotsit, *I* want to be one as well!'

'Well you can't, and that's final,' replied his mum, rolling out some barbed wire and carefully placing it around the playpen. 'Right. That should keep you in,' she announced, heading towards the door.

'Now, Hodge, be a good boy and play with the nice moon rocks I got you.' And she closed the door behind her, locking and bolting it.

Immediately, Hodge set to work. He pulled up the carpet, grabbed hold of his rattle and began tunnelling under the floorboards. A faded pink toy rabbit,

which had been lying in the corner, joined him. He had extremely long legs and ears, his name was Rotten Rabbit, and he was Hodge's favourite toy.

'OK, Rotten, start digging,' he said, handing the bunny a toy spade.

Rotten Rabbit jumped down into the hole, and, discarding the spade, he began to burrow away with his paws, scattering bits of earth all over his friend.

'Well, bless my hutch!' he said, 'I do declare we've almost reached the living room door.'

Hodge clapped his hands delightedly. He and Rotten Rabbit had been working day and night to secretly tunnel their way out of the playpen prison and now they'd almost made it.

Quickly, Hodge put all his belongings into a bag: his rattle and bottle, a large supply of dummies, a couple of clean nappies, and a pair of braces with spaceships printed on them. Hodge always wore braces attached to his nappies, otherwise they tended to fall down. He also packed a plentiful supply of his favourite baby food called Slop. It tasted even worse than it sounded, but Hodge thought it was delicious. He gave the bag to Rotten Rabbit and then they set off down the tunnel.

When they reached the living room door they stopped for a quick nap and then began digging again.

Half an hour later they emerged out the other side and into the hallway. Hodge looked down the corridor. His high powered pushchair was standing by the front door. It was an incredible looking machine, with big fat wheels, lots of shiny chrome and a dashboard covered with knobs and dials. From the hood hung two gigantic fluffy dice and on the back was a sticker that read *BAD BABY ON BOARD*. It was the most powerful pushchair in the whole universe and Hodge dribbled excitedly down the front of his playsuit when he spotted it. Rotten had to mop him up with a tissue.

Passing the kitchen they could see Hodge's mum's feet under the table as she sat eating her lunch, and very quietly they tiptoed past. When they reached the front

door Hodge climbed on to Rotten's back and carefully opened it. Jumping down, he scrambled into the pushchair and Rotten Rabbit pushed it outside.

Ghastly, the most garish, tasteless planet in the whole universe was, as usual, in full swing. Neon lights flashed on and off maniacally from every building, pavement slab and street corner. In fact, the whole planet resembled an enormous disco, and with everyone rushing around dressed in the most outrageous clothes and chatting away to each other, nobody took any notice of a little boy and his toy rabbit heading out of town.

Hodge could hardly contain his excitement as they reached the outskirts and he revved up his pushchair, putting it into gear. Almost immediately it shot up into the sky, taking off with Rotten Rabbit swinging from side to side like a piece of rag as Hodge steered.

'Woo! Woo! Woo! It's a carrot calamity.

Where are we heading, Hodgy baby?' he asked, his long ears fluttering out behind him as Hodge put his foot down hard on the accelerator and speeded up.

Hodge whooped with delight. 'We're heading for earth, Rotten Rabbit!' he hollered, as the pushchair swerved to the right, hit two thousand miles an hour on the speedometer and shot off into deepest space with Hodge's words, 'IT'S PLAYTIME!!!!' reverberating around the solar system.

Two

Seymour Potts turned down the TV set and strained his super-sensitive ears to listen. The words were faint, but he'd definitely heard something. Seymour stuck his head out of the window and looked up into the sky. It was empty, except for a few clouds dotted about. But then he heard it again, and this time there was no mistake. The voice was louder now but still very far away and it said 'IT'S PLAYTIME!!' as clear as day.

Seymour hurried up to his bedroom. It was currently being decorated and all his belongings, including his pet ants and collection of sweet wrappers, had been moved. Seymour sat down on a paint can,

pulled his Magnificent Misfit mobile from his pocket and dialled Omonoslomo's number. It took a while to connect, because the planet Twart where their leader lived, was ten thousand light years away but after a few clicks and buzzes he finally got through.

The voice of Omonoslomo's robot

crackled over the line: 'Omonoslomo's residence. Pickthank speaking. How may I help you?'

'Hello, Pickthank. It's Seymour Misfit here. How are you?' said Seymour in his usual friendly manner. He could hear Pickthank whirring and clanking down the phone. The battered old robot sounded as if he were falling apart.

'I've got a bit of a cold actually,' he replied, sniffing into the mouthpiece. 'And I could do with a holiday, but Omonoslomo's got a 'Masters of the Universe' convention coming up so I can't go anywhere. Hold on. I'll just get him for you.' And he went whirring off. A moment later Omonoslomo came on the line and Seymour explained about what he'd just heard.

'It sounds like Hodge the Little Horror, that terrible toddler I warned you about, is on his way,' declared Omonoslomo seriously. 'Even though he's only two years old and hasn't been on the Universe's 'Most Wanted' list for long, don't underestimate him, Seymour Misfit.'

'The Magnificent Misfits will be on full alert,' replied Seymour, trying to sound efficient. He knew that Omonoslomo was aware of the mistakes they'd made already, so they couldn't afford to make any more.

'Good,' said his leader firmly. 'Because I'm off to a meeting tomorrow that's headed by Dr K, the most powerful leader in the whole universe. He also happens to be in charge of the hiring, not to mention *firing* of all superheroes. He'll be asking me about your progress, Seymour, and I'll cover for you as best I can, but the Magnificent Misfits will have to shape up, otherwise you, me *and* Pickthank will *all* be out of a job. Is that clear? Over and out.'

Seymour bit his bottom lip nervously. The last thing he wanted was to let Omonoslomo down. He sighed heavily. He really didn't want to go back to being

Seymour Potts, picked-on school kid again. As a Magnificent Misfit he finally felt he was *somebody*. Not a joke, nor a dimwit and always the last one over the finishing line on sports day.

Suddenly, Seymour's phone rang. It was Timothy Elastic, another of the Magnificent Misfits. He hoped Timothy wasn't ringing to have a moan. He and his twin brother Keith were good at that, especially now they were superheroes and had to work long hours without getting paid.

Seymour frowned into the mouthpiece. It sounded very noisy in the background, and he hoped that they were taking care of the precious pickled onion jar that he'd given them to look after while he was having his bedroom decorated.

'Mrs Checkocheck's roped us into helping with our next-door neighbour's kid's birthday party.' shouted Timothy over the noise. 'It's terrible, Seymour. I've had jelly shoved down the back of my jumper, a soda syphon squirted up my nose and I've been bitten on the ear by a baby. I think I might need stitches! This is no job for a superhero!' he wailed.

'Well I'm sorry, Timothy,' replied Seymour, looking despondently around his bare room. 'But what can I do about it?' Seymour didn't mean to sound rude, but he had far more pressing things on his mind, like the arrival of a terrible toddler from outer space, and whether his beloved ants were safe in the garage.

'Listen, Seymour. Something very odd has happened,' continued Timothy, ignoring him. 'A little kid's turned up on the doorstep in a pushchair. He's all alone except for a tatty toy rabbit that won't stop yakking, and now he's demanding ice-cream.'

'Big deal, Timothy,' sighed Seymour, rolling his eyes in exasperation. 'Perhaps his mum's left him there in a hurry. The

toy probably runs on batteries and all kids love ice-cream. There's nothing weird about that.'

Timothy took a deep breath. 'But his name's *Hodge*, Seymour! Remember Omonoslomo and that passport controller on Ghastly warned us about him. Only he's not asking for any old ice-cream. He's demanding *pickled onion* flavoured ice-cream. Now don't you think *that's* peculiar?'

Suddenly Timothy let out a loud yelp.

'Timothy! Whatever's happened?' cried Seymour anxiously, leaping up and knocking over the paint can as he realised exactly who his friend was talking about. 'Has Hodge the Little Horror done something to you?'

'No!' wailed Timothy, blubbing into the phone. 'That blasted baby's gone and bitten me on the other ear this time!'

Three

Seymour quickly changed out of his ordinary clothes and into his lime green Misfit costume, then he rushed downstairs to find his sister Elsie, the youngest of the Magnificent Misfits. She was playing in the garden with Gladys, her pretend friend, and he told her what had happened.

'Come on, Elsie. We've got to get to the twin's flat,' said Seymour, hustling her inside and pacing up and down the patio as he waited for his sister to change. Their mum was due back soon and he was anxious not to bump into her, because even though no one was supposed to recognise them when they were wearing their Misfit disguises, Seymour didn't want to take any chances. It would be really terrible if his mum ever found out that he and his sister were real-life superheroes. She'd tell all the neighbours, her friends down at the slimming club, even the woman who worked in the newsagents, probably. His mum loved to chat, and she never could keep a secret.

Finally Elsie emerged and they raced off, clutching their Miskit boxes under their arms. When they were safely out of sight they pulled out their Space Hoppers, inflated them and flew off in the direction of Arkwright House, which was where the Elastic twins lived.

As they landed on a patch of grass behind the flats, they could see that Barrington Small and Fabian Farquar, two of the other Misfits were already waiting. Standing alongside them was a familiar spotty face. It was Ninian Soames, superhero expert and all round nosy parker.

You could bet your life that wherever Fabian was, Ninian was never far behind. Ninian had had his doubts about the authenticity of the Magnificent Misfits from the very first day he'd met them, and he was particularly suspicious about Fabian. Who'd ever heard of a superhero doing his washing all day long? Ninian lightly fingered Fabian's suit as he looked for tell-tale clues. Perhaps a speck of moon dust, or a few scorch marks from the sun. There was nothing, for Fabian Farquar was the cleanest superhero to ever walk the planet. Fabian tutted crossly. 'Please keep your mucky paws off my suit. It's just been washed.' He frowned at Ninian and then gathering up his Miskit box, he hurried after the others as they made their way towards the entrance to the flats.

Once inside, they squeezed into the lift and travelled up to the third floor. As they emerged, they spotted the Elastic twins coming out of their flat.

'We slipped away from the party to get changed,' said Keith, doing up his Misfit outfit, which was far too big for him. 'It's murder in there. Hodge has been spoiling everything. He's upset the birthday boy and opened all of his presents, except the one that he bought him.'

'Well at least he gave him a present. That was thoughtful,' said Barrington, who always tried to see the best in everyone.

'Not really,' replied Keith. 'It was a toolkit complete with a drill, saw, and some lethal-looking nails. The kid's only two years old and he was just about to smash his mum's best china with the hammer when she spotted him. Hodge has also been very rude to Mrs Checkocheck and called her Mrs Big Bum twice. I don't know how he found us, but I bet his Uncle Vince has got something to do with it.'

'Oh dear. I don't like the sound of this,' replied Fabian, staring nervously at the others and knocking on the door of number twelve. He didn't like little children, they tended to dribble a lot and spit and he shuddered at the thought of being surrounded by them.

A very harassed-looking young woman, who looked like she'd been wrestling with a herd of rhino, opened the front door.

'Oh. Thank goodness you've arrived!' she gushed, dragging them inside.

'I booked a clown to entertain my son actually, but never mind, you Magnificent Misfit lookalikes will do instead.' And she pushed Seymour and the others into the living room.

The place was in chaos. Children of all shapes and sizes were running riot. There were cake crumbs on the carpet, sandwiches stuffed down the sofa and the curtains were soaked in lemonade. Hodge the Little Horror stood in the middle of the room, swinging Rotten Rabbit by one arm and eating a slice of birthday cake that was bigger than his face. He'd poured some Slop over it and it was now dripping all over the carpet.

The lady pointed towards him. 'There's the culprit,' she declared crossly. 'Everything was under control until he turned up. Right little savage he is. I've no idea where the little devil comes from. But

I hope his mum arrives to collect him soon. I certainly don't want my Troy mixing with the likes of him.'

She stared at The Magnificent Misfits. 'Shouldn't you be singing or dancing or something?' she asked indignantly. 'After all, that's what I paid for.'

Seymour smiled and considered telling her that they were actually *real* superheroes, and that Hodge was in fact an alien from the planet Ghastly who was after the most powerful pickles in the solar system, but he decided against it. Troy's mum looked like she'd had enough shocks for one day.

'Perhaps we could play a game or something?' Suggested Barrington brightly. 'Pass the Parcel maybe? I like that, even if I don't ever win.'

Troy's mum nodded eagerly. 'My neighbour Mrs Checkocheck is organising that,' she replied. 'Actually. I think she's already wrapped something up. Her two sons were supposed to be helping her, but they've disappeared. Right couple of moaners they are as well. I don't know why she ever adopted them.'

The Elastic twins glared at her beneath their baggy hoods.

'Cheek,' muttered Keith under his breath.

'Sauce,' added Timothy under his.

'Anyway,' continued Troy's mum, watching Hodge climb on to the table, using a little girl's plaits to pull himself up. 'I just hope the poor dear can see what she's doing. Unfortunately she lost her glasses earlier and she's as blind as a bat without them.'

Just then Mrs Checkocheck came out of the kitchen squinting and smiling like a startled mole. In her hand she held a big fat parcel and she padded over towards the Magnificent Misfits.

'I found a nice jar of sweets on the side, so I wrapped them up,' she announced,

handing the package to Barrington.

Troy's mum frowned. 'Sweets? What jar of sweets?' she asked staring at the package. 'You were supposed to wrap up a jigsaw puzzle.'

The Magnificent Misfits followed her gaze, Seymour frowning at the parcel's familiar shape.

'What have you done with the onions, Timothy?' he hissed, fearing the worst. Keith and Timothy stared blankly at each other. 'Well. We brought them with us earlier, just to be on the safe side, but then we left them in the kitchen when we went to change into our Misfit costumes,' said Keith. 'We were only gone for a moment. Timothy said no one would take any notice of a boring old jar. He put it between the tins marked Tea and Coffee.'

Timothy shrugged. 'How was I to know Mrs Checkocheck would use them for a Pass the Parcel prize. They're pickled onions, for goodness sake!'

'Sssh! Keep your voice down!' whispered Seymour, looking over his shoulder. Hodge the Little Horror was standing directly behind them, listening intently. His eyes narrowed and he pulled his dummy out of his mouth with a pop and handed it to Rotten Rabbit.

'You got doze pickles?' he demanded,

stamping his foot and pointing at the parcel.

Barrington shook his head and hid them behind his back. 'Pickles? What pickles?' he laughed nervously, as Troy's mum put on a CD and everyone sat in a circle to begin the game. As the music started, Barrington quickly passed the parcel on, and Hodge chased after it around the outside of the ring. When the music stopped, Troy was left holding the package.

'Yippee!' he cried ecstatically. It was the first present he'd been able to open all day apart from the deadly toolkit.

'Mine!' declared Hodge, snatching it out of his hands and tearing at the paper.

Troy's mum quickly turned the music up again. But Hodge wouldn't let go. He gripped the package with fists of iron until Elsie finally managed to prise it away from him.

Round and round, and faster and faster

it continued to go, until the music stopped again, this time at Barrington.

'Brilliant,' declared Barrington, excitedly ripping the paper. 'This could be my lucky day.' But he'd only got down a layer when the music began, and once again he had to pass it on.

'Mine!' demanded Hodge, pushing in

and grabbing the parcel from the girl with the plaits.

'Mine!' snapped Fabian, snatching it back.

'Mine!' declared Keith, wrenching it away.

'It's mine!' said Timothy, seizing it from his brother.

'I think you'll find it's mine, actually,' replied Seymour, pulling at it with all his strength. The other children in the circle watched in amazement as the Magnificent Misfits squabbled amongst themselves like big baby superheroes fighting over a toy.

'But I had it first,' declared Barrington, tugging on the wrapping paper so hard that he fell backwards. The pickled onion jar suddenly flew out of Seymour's hands, shot across the room and hurtled straight out of an open window.

'Whoops! Silly me!' declared Barrington, as he and the others ran over to the window.

They were just in time to see the jar land on top of a double decker bus, and with a flying leap Barrington jumped straight out of the window after it, landing with a thud on the roof just as the bus pulled away.

'Good job I remembered to take my Power Powder this morning,' he shouted, as the bus gathered speed and he wobbled about in his bright pink Misfit suit, trying to keep his balance. Barrington's special power as a Magnificent Misfit was to be as agile as a cat, but as Seymour watched his friend rocking from side to side like a surfer on a huge red wave, he was beginning to have his doubts.

'You've forgotten your Miskit!' cried Seymour, holding up Barrington's case that contained his Space Hopper and various other superhero items, but Barrington couldn't hear over the roar of the traffic.

As he and the other Misfits turned away from the window, they saw Hodge and

Rotten Rabbit backing out of the front door with the pushchair.

Troy's mum let out a cry as she saw that strapped inside it, with a party hat pulled firmly down over his head, was the birthday boy himself.

'The party's over. Stay where you are,' threatened Hodge, dragging the pushchair out on to the balcony. 'One false move and the kid gets it,' and he held his dummy out in front of him menacingly.

'Don't be a fool. Put the dummy down, Hodge,' said Seymour, moving slowly towards him and eyeing it suspiciously. The dummy was pink plastic and looked ordinary enough, but then the strangest thing began to happen. It started to grow at an alarming rate and just got bigger and bigger until eventually it filled the whole doorway, plugging it up like a gigantic mouth, trapping everyone inside.

The Magnificent Misfits had no time to lose. From the window they could see

Rotten Rabbit emerging from the flats, pushing the pushchair with Hodge the Little Horror now sitting on top of poor Troy's head.

'Do something! He's squashing my boy!' wailed Troy's mum, as Seymour and the others hastily opened up their Miskits, pulled out their deflated Space Hoppers and quickly blew them up. Then one by one they climbed out on to the window ledge and took off in pursuit of the number 13 bus, the tiny tearaway and his bad, bad bunny.

Four

'Oi! 'ave you paid your fare?' The bus conductor leant out of his bus and frowned up at Barrington, who didn't reply. The bus was travelling very fast and he was concentrating extremely hard on keeping his balance. The jar had slid all the way up to the front of the bus now, and Barrington knew that with one false move, it would go over the top and certainly be smashed to smithereens.

'I SAID, 'AVE YOU PAID YOUR FARE!' The conductor was getting very cross now.

Barrington peered cautiously down at him. 'I'm terribly sorry,' he replied carefully, trying to make his way along the slippery roof. 'But I don't have any money

on me. I'm a superhero, you see, and I'm on a very important world-saving mission.'

The conductor leant further out. 'Yeah. And I'm Batman. This is just my day job!' He glared up at Barrington. 'Now listen. Superhero or not, either pay your fare or get off my bus.' And with that he rang the bell a few times and the bus skidded to a halt.

Barrington immediately lost his balance, fell forward and slid along the roof towards the jar. It teetered on the edge for a moment and then toppled off. Barrington made a grab for it, but missed and he watched despairingly as the pickles fell towards the ground. But then suddenly, a motorbike swerved in front of the bus and the jar dropped straight into a metal box attached to the back.

Barrington jumped down from the roof, as the bike took off up the road, and raced over to a little girl who was sitting on a small plastic bike, waiting patiently to cross the road with her mum. He lifted her off and plonked her down on the pavement.

'Please excuse me,' he announced politely, 'but I need to borrow your bike.' And to the little girl's astonishment, he climbed on to it and peddled off, hunched over the handlebars with his knees banging against his chin.

Overhead, Hodge the Little Horror dipped and dived in his pushchair.

'Hey nice wheels man! *Not!*' cried Rotten Rabbit with a grin. He looked over his shoulder as the other Magnificent Misfits gained on them. 'Woo! Woo! Woo! It's a carrot calamity, Hodgy baby,' he exclaimed. 'Put your foot down on the gas, kid. The Misfits are a comin'.'

Hodge's pushchair gathered speed, as the motorbike turned into a driveway and went through some big double gates. Barrington peddled frantically after it. The driveway led into an enormous garden, with a marquee tent, a bandstand and lots of smartly-dressed people milling around. Barrington realised that they'd arrived at a wedding reception, because standing right in the middle of the lawn was a big woman wearing an even bigger dress. It was white and wide with a long net train that circled the top of her head, travelled down her back, and finished up curled around the fishpond. Standing beside her was her tiny husband, who was lost inside an enormous top hat.

Barrington tiptoed behind a nearby clump of bushes and peeped through as

the man on the motorbike climbed off, unclipped the box and carried it over to the wedding party. He turned out to be the photographer, because a moment later, he pulled a camera out and proceeded to take a few snaps.

Suddenly, Barrington heard a rustling sound behind him and he turned around to see the other Misfits trample out through the bushes.

'Where's the jar?' whispered Seymour, pulling some twigs from his hood and bending down beside his friend. Barrington pointed to the man's box.

Seymour nodded. 'And Hodge?'

This time Barrington indicated towards a group of waiters standing around. In amongst them, holding a tray full of drinks, were Hodge and Rotten Rabbit. Rotten Rabbit had tied his ears up with a napkin to disguise himself, but he still looked suspiciously like a rabbit. The Magnificent Misfits watched them as they

began handing out drinks. When they reached the photographer, he peered down at Hodge.

'You're very small for a waiter,' he remarked, picking up a glass. 'And your friend looks a bit pink as well. Has he been out in the sun too long?'

The man frowned at Rotten, who frowned back. Then he let out a little squeal, and so did Rotten. 'You're a rabbit!' he exclaimed, dropping his glass. Everyone turned around.

Rotten Rabbit stared at him, his nose twitching rapidly. 'Alrighdy mister! Keep your hair on. Haven't you ever seen a bunny before!'

The man shook his head.

'Not working as a waiter, I haven't,' he replied indignantly. Then he pointed at Hodge. 'And he's not a grown-up. He's a baby!' he exclaimed, barely able to conceal his excitement.

'Yeah. And I'm the baddest baby that

ever toddled. Now give me doze pickles,' demanded Hodge, placing his hands firmly on his hips and scowling at the man.

The man stared blankly at him. 'I don't *have* any pickles. I don't even *like* pickles.' He patted Hodge gingerly on the top of his wispy head. 'Now run along, sonny. Take your bunny and go find your mummy. There's a good boy.'

Hodge was fuming. If there was one thing he hated, apart from when his mum called him Pudding Pie, it was being patted on the top of his head.

He jumped up and down a few times to show how cross he really was.

'Woo! Woo! Woo! It's a carrot catastrophe,' declared Rotten shaking his head woefully. 'You've made him *really* angry now.'

From the bushes the Misfits watched as Hodge the little Horror whipped out a rattle from the waistband of his nappy and

twirled it high above his head. It made a
whooshing sound like the wind, and
suddenly metal objects began to be drawn
towards it like a magnet. People sitting on
metal chairs began bumping across the
grass towards him. The tent pegs holding
up the marquee flew out, tin trays spun

through the air like frisbees, keys were sucked out of pockets, even the bride's tiara was torn off.

The Magnificent Misfits raced across the lawn towards Hodge, as the instruments from the brass band went whizzing past their ears and a tambourine landed on top of Timothy's head.

Finally, Hodge stopped waving the rattle around and beside him there now stood an enormous pile of objects, including chairs, tables, a trombone and even a small car. Hodge dragged the photographer's metal box from beneath a lawnmower.

'I told you to give me doze pickles,' he said, tipping it upside down and shaking it. The man's cameras and tripod fell on to the lawn along with the pickled onion jar. The Magnificent Misfits gasped as it began to roll across the lawn, bouncing towards the fishpond.

'Follow that jar!' cried Seymour, pointing towards the runaway pickles.

The bride shrieked as the jar took a slight turn to the right, narrowly missing the pond, and rolled beneath her enormous gown. It was closely followed by Seymour, Elsie, Hodge and Rotten, as in a flurry of petticoats they pursued the precious pickles and crawled out the other side.

'Well bless my hutch!' said Rotten, glancing at the crowd over his shoulder. 'I do declare she was wearing the biggest pair of knickers I've *ever* seen!'

'Help!' squealed the new bride as she rocked from side to side like an enormous bell, trying to keep her balance, and finally falling flat on her face in the fishpond. Her husband peered out from beneath his top hat, while he and the other guests watched in amazement as the jar rolled on and inside the wobbly marquee with the two Misfits, the teeny terror and Rotten in hot pursuit. Barrington brought up the rear and was just about to follow the others inside when he tripped over the last-remaining tent peg. The guy rope snapped and the enormous structure billowed once like a gigantic soufflé and then sank slowly to the ground around their ears.

The fight continued beneath the voluminous cloth, with clouds of dust and dirt being kicked up everywhere and bulges popping up from every conceivable

angle. Occasionally a foot or paw would appear, and then Rotten's face popped out, framed in silky white cloth. His ears had fallen down and he fanned his flustered face with them.

'This is no life for a rabbit,' he exclaimed. 'I should be nibbling on a celery stick, or filing my teeth, not squabbling over some onions with so-called superheroes!'

Suddenly, Rotten's ears began to tremble and his long teeth began to chatter, as Elsie, who had the power to shout louder than anyone in the whole universe, let out an earth-shattering cry. It was so loud it made everyone within a five-mile radius stop in their tracks. A moment later, Elsie emerged triumphantly holding the jar. As the tent stopped quivering from the shock waves, the others, staggered out after her. Seymour looked stunned. He'd been right next to his sister when she'd decided to let rip and now his ears with their incredible hearing power were ringing like fifty

thousand alarm bells. Everyone was filthy, and Fabian, in his dazzling suit, was glad that he hadn't become involved in such a messy brawl.

The bride herself was a sorry state. She'd been fished out of the pond and was soaked from head to foot. She had a slimy piece of weed stuck down the front of her dress and her hair looked as if it had been styled with a pitchfork.

'I've heard all about you so-called superheroes,' complained the bride's mother, scowling at the Magnificent Misfits and lightly patting her daughter's podgy hand. 'You took away my friend's tennis racket last week.'

'Well, some things can be very dangerous in the wrong hands,' replied Barrington seriously.

'But she's fifty-six and wouldn't hurt a fly!' declared the woman crossly.

Seymour and the others smiled sheepishly at her, remembering the very posh lady they'd stopped outside the sports centre last Friday.

Soon, everyone began to gather around with various superhero-saving complaints. Then Seymour's mobile rang and he quickly answered it.

'I'm sorry to bother you,' a voice came

over the line. 'But I got your number from Omonoslomo. I'm Hodge's mum. Is he there, by any chance?'

'Hold on one moment,' replied Seymour with surprise. 'It's for you,' he declared, handing the phone to Hodge, who snatched it from him.

'Pudding Pie!' Cried his Mum. 'There you are, you naughty boy. Guess what your mummy has got for you?'

'Dunno.' replied Hodge with a shrug. He still had one eye on the pickled onion jar and was planning his next move.

'Remember that rocket I ordered for you from the catalogue? Well it's arrived. The postman's left it on the front lawn. You'll love it, Hodge, it's just what you always wanted.' A slight smile began to flicker across Hodge's face, and then he glared at everyone as they began bickering amongst themselves again.

'SHUT-UP!!' he bawled. 'Show some manners. My mum's on the phone.'

Everyone stopped and listened intently to Hodge's conversation.

'Is it the super-fuelled one with the silver fins that we saw in the picture?' he asked eagerly.

'The very same,' declared Hodge's mum proudly.

'In racing red?'

'Uh huh,' she replied.

'Carpeted throughout?'

'From top to bottom.'

'What about a bed?'

'Bunkbeds,' announced his mum firmly. 'One for you and one for Rotten.'

Rotten gave Hodge the thumbs-up. He wanted to go home to a nice big slice of Hodge's mum's carrot quiche.

Hodge thought for a moment. 'What about a fridge for my jars of Slop?'

'All included, along with a microwave,' said Hodge's mum enticingly.

'Sky?'

'Fifty-two channels. You can't do better

than that,' she declared adamantly. Hodge
chomped thoughtfully on a dummy for a
moment and then stuck it behind his ear.

'Right Mum,' he said finally. 'Put me
dinner on. I'm on my way.'

Rotten Rabbit hurried off to get his
pushchair, and returned a moment later

pushing it over the bumpy lawn with poor Troy bouncing about, still strapped inside. He looked very bewildered, especially when Hodge pulled him out and tossed him up in the air. Luckily, Fabian caught him and he held him gingerly, while Troy got chocolate finger marks all over his nice clean Misfit costume.

Everyone watched as Hodge climbed into his pushchair and prepared for take-off.

'Now, go home and get your nappy changed,' said Seymour firmly.

The Elastic twins sniffed the air, with their super-smelling noses and nodded in agreement.

Hodge sneered at the Misfits. 'You can keep your stupid old world. It's boring anyway,' he replied, settling himself in the pushchair as Rotten strapped him in. 'There's a whole galaxy to explore out there and now I've got my rocket I can go anywhere.'

He revved up his engine. 'Who knows, though. One day this baby might be back.' And he popped his dummy into his mouth, shot off into the sky and disappeared behind a large cloud.

After a while, the photographer announced that he was late for a christening, so everyone gathered around to have a last picture taken. The dishevelled bride and her groom in the middle, the parents either side, and the Magnificent Misfits standing proudly on tiptoe at the back.

Troy's mum turned up to collect him and to return Barrington's Miskit. The little girl whose bicycle Barrington had borrowed, also arrived with her mum. Barrington shook his head gravely at her. 'I'm very sorry, but I'm afraid I'll have to confiscate this bike,' he announced seriously.

The little girl stared at him wide eyed. 'Why? Is it dangerous?' she asked in bewilderment.

Barrington nodded solemnly. 'The bell doesn't work properly. It gives a *ping* instead of a *ding*, when it really should give a *ring*.'

Tears welled up in the girl's eyes. 'But I love that bike,' she replied.

Barrington peered down at her and sighed. 'OK. Call me a big softy. I'll let you take it home. Only get a new bell for it, because my fellow Misfits and I shall be keeping an eye out for you. Is that clear?'

The little girl nodded and went off, pulling her bike along behind her.

The Magnificent Misfits set off up the driveway. They'd decided to walk home, because blowing up their Space Hoppers all the time was getting very tiring. The streets were deserted and only the odd net curtain twitched as they passed the houses. Word was spreading fast about these interfering superheroes.

'Another successful day,' announced Seymour, as they strolled on regardless.

The others nodded. Everyone agreed that being a superhero, even if you weren't a very good one, was brilliant. And when they reached the end of the street they linked arms and proudly sang this song:

'WHO'S THE BRAVEST BUNCH OF ALL?
SAVING PEOPLE BIG AND SMALL?
WHEN YOU NEED HELP, WE'LL
    ALWAYS RISK IT.
WHAT'S OUR NAME?
THE MAGNIFICENT MISFITS!!'